MW00944728

Diary of an
Angry Alex: Book 2

By **Crafty Nichole**

All rights reserved.

This book is copyright protected and intended for personal use only. You may not copy, share, sell, or quote any part of or any content within this book without the full consent of the author, publishing company. Making copies of these pages or any portion for any purpose other than your personal use is a violation of United States copyright laws.

This handbook is for entertainment purposes only and is a complete work of fiction.

This handbook is not official and has no association with the makers of Minecraft.

All references to Minecraft, its characters and other trademarked properties are used in accordance to the Fair Use Doctrine.

Minecraft is a trademark of Mojang AB, Sweden

Minecraft ®/TM & © 2009-2015 Mojang / Notch

Contents

Contents

Day Sixteen

9:00am

I mined all day yesterday and it was awesome! Steve is pretty great for understanding that I need a change of scenery. I only found gold yesterday, but Steve encouraged me to keep looking, because where there is gold, there are diamonds -- or so he says. Down in the mines I can be myself and feel free to explore our world.

11:30am

Diamonds! I discovered three this morning. Maybe I'll go back later and hunt for more. Steve congratulated me and said finding diamonds takes patience, and I just have to keep at it.

Steve also complained another creeper blew out one side of the pig fence. I think he is a little sore he had to fix it. I know creepers are frustrating -- poor Steve.

11:45am

The wreckage left behind by creeper was worse than I imagined. Steve's repair attempts left a few weak spots. He frowned and stomped off when I pointed them out. I was just trying to be helpful…

12:50pm

I mended the pig pen, but I didn't tell Steve. Hopefully, no more creepers ruin his day.

1:00pm

Steve noticed my repair job. He got furious and told me that he is perfectly capable of fixing things and to mind my own business. That's the last time I try and help.

2:05pm

I made a diamond pickaxe. I turned it over in my hands watching it glitter in the sunlight. It's the most beautiful thing I have ever owned and was a definite improvement over my iron ore tools. I remembered Steve instructing me to use diamond pickaxe to mine obsidian, which is rarer than iron ore, so I would only need one diamond pickaxe and many iron ones. I have to admit he knows more than I do when it comes to mining.

4:30pm

I asked Steve for help enchanting my pickaxe. He exclaimed he had no time and rushed back towards the crops looking frazzled. He is the pro at mining, but he doesn't seem to have the hang of farming yet. I have long been a pro at farming and harvesting. I can fend off spiders, dodge creepers, and knock out the chores. I could teach Steve a thing or two.

6:10pm

When Steve returned, I offered some farming advice. He said he knows what he's doing and will be just fine.

4:00am

I just spent all night mining! I enjoy it so much I lose track of time. I came across an endless supply of lava and water. I experimented for hours and finally figured out how to make obsidian. I am pretty proud of myself, but I'm not sure what I'm supposed to do with this chest stuffed with cobblestone, andesite, diorite, and granite. What am I supposed to do with all of this rock?

Day Seventeen

10:00am

It's pouring rain. I passed Steve as I sloshed through the mud to the mines. I waved but I'm not sure he noticed. He was busy battling zombies while trying to plant carrots. I thought I heard him growl. Has he learned to speak zombie? Good luck, Steve. Those things are mean!

3:45pm

I busted about a mountain-worth of rocks today. I think I'd better start creating with all I've mined. But it's hard to make myself stop mining. I have been working so much that it seems that diamonds should be falling out of my pockets by now. Not even close. I didn't even find one! Instead, I have a chest full of stupid Lapis Lazuli. Who needs that much Lapis anyway?

4:00pm

When Steve saw my Lapis collection, he was equally unimpressed. Maybe I could use it for ground cover in our rock garden. Steve wasn't interested in discussing the possibilities but went straight to his room. It's a little early for sleep I'd say.

5:30pm

I baked a Steve a cherry pie and, while it was still steaming, carried it to his room. He told me was going to bed and wouldn't accept it. Weird... Steve loves pie! He just asked me to leave and said he was tired and going to bed. At 5:30? Is he really that tired? Or is he mad?

6:15pm

I used 34 lapis lazuli used to enchant my armor with a protection enchantment. I looked in the mirror, dazzled by the effect. I also enchanted three of my swords. I feel invincible!

Only 192 lapis left in my chest. I am going to enchant EVERYTHING! Yikes. As I wrote this, I let out one of my evil laughs, which still sounds too much like a donkey. I need to make an appointment with a speech therapist.

6:30pm

I've been trying to enchant Ruby, Steve's pet cat. She's an ocelot, but the wild has gone out of her and she is pretty much just a house cat now.

7:00pm

I can't get the enchantment to work. I just want to make Ruby fire resistant. She keeps scratching me and running away. I guess she doesn't appreciate the tests I need to do to see of the enchantment was effective. I need to go find the air freshener to get the burnt cat fur smell out of the house.

9:00pm

Steve seems pretty miffed about Ruby. I can't work on the enchantment anymore because Steve shut himself in his room with her. I hope he's okay.

Day Eighteen

8:00am

I woke up while it was still dark. I felt bad about harassing Ruby. So I decided to use all my extra rocks to build a place for her to play. I worked for hours before presenting it to Steve and Ruby. Steve thanked me, but he wasn't sure Ruby would use it. Sure enough, Ruby sniffed at it with disdain and then went to nap on Steve's bed. Oh well... I think it looks cool. Maybe I'll sit on top of it and shoot zombies with my arrow when I'm bored.

12:00pm

I stumbled upon an abandoned mineshaft this morning and found an old chest with a handful of gold and oodles of diamonds. Finally... diamonds! I filled my pockets before exploring the rest of the mine shaft.

That's where I got bit. Spiders are the absolute worst, and I think these spiders were poisonous.

They all came out of a flaming cage, just like the zombies did! I scrambled in my panic, searching my brain for the right thing to do, but my mind wouldn't work right as my hearts went "tick, tick, tick" each

7

time I was stung. As reason overcame my panic, I realized that pain of the stings was the least of my worries. I was quickly dying from poison.

I re-spawned in bed, dizzy and confused. My head was pounding. Dying leaves you with such a headache! It was finally going so great, and now I have nothing to show for it.

Worst of all, I was all the way to Level 38... Level 38! Now, I am back to zero. So much for working on my enchantments -- it's back to busting rocks.

12:15pm

When I told Steve all about my morning, he laughed! Not cool, Steve.

12:30pm

Steve suggested crafting a brewing stand so that I can make health potions for when I am poisoned. I asked Steve why I couldn't just use his brewing stand. He snapped that that stand was his and I couldn't use it. Fine, then. Be that way.

3:10pm

Steve didn't finish harvesting this morning because few lingering endermen. They really scare him. I decided to help him finish, but he didn't even say thank you. Rude.

6:00pm

Dinner tonight was delicious. Mutton chops, mushroom soup -- my favorites! Steve just pushed away his untouched plate of chops and went to bed. Something is definitely up with Steve.

8:15pm

I knocked on Steve's door and offered to switch our jobs back tomorrow. His face lit up with a tremendous grin like a big old pumpkin. Maybe the harvesting is too much for him. I can't blame him. I felt the same way my first harvest. A day back in the fields should help with his moodiness.

Day Nineteen

10:00am

Just my luck! Just one hour back with the crops and along came a creeper with its warning hiss. I ran away just in time, but he got half the potato plot. Dirt, wood, and potatoes are scattered haphazardly. What a mess! Why do these wretched creatures exist? They're nothing but camouflaged, exploding menaces and are downright annoying. I'll be rebuilding this mess all day. Hopefully Steve is enjoying the mines. A more cheerful Steve will make it all worth it.

2:45pm

Rebuilding didn't take as long as I thought it would, but just when things seemed under control, I accidently let a sheep out. I wore myself out chasing the fluffy critter before remembering to pull out my wheat and lure it back to the pen. I forgot how hard farming is! I'm a sweaty mess. The sheep looks proud of itself. Stupid sheep…

4:10pm

Steve is back with a large haul of diamonds. He says he just found them floating above the ground in a mine. I'll bet he was where I ran into the spiders. When I asked him for a few jewels, he cracked up laughing and told me not a chance. To think I'd felt sorry for him! My dislike for Steve returned with a vengeance.

7:30pm

Without a word of thanks, Steve wolfed down dinner and, once again, shut himself in his room. I could hear scuffles of mysterious activity behind his door, but I couldn't tell what he was up to.

8:00pm

I guess Steve is cleaning out his room. He just gave me an old pair of well-worn diamond boots. They had no sheen left to speak of. Gee, thanks, Steve…

8:02pm

Steve also asked to go back to the mine tomorrow. Were the boots a bribe? Ugh! I guess I will let him, but only because he seems happier – though not any nicer. I guess that would be too much to ask for.

11:59pm

I went to bed a few hours ago but woke up in a sweat. I had a dream I was a creeper and exploded! I had never thought about how sad a creeper's life must be. Poor dudes!

Day Twenty

6:45pm

I'm exhausted. I spent far too long thinking of creeper's tragic lives instead of sleeping. Maybe if they sparked up a conversation with me sometimes instead of exploding, I could start a creeper therapy group. Hmm…

So much work to do today! My to-do list includes harvesting, breeding some cows, and dying some sheep. Where to start? Hopefully, my sleepy brain won't have me dying the cows and harvesting the sheep.

10:00am

I hope Steve is having more fun than I am. The harvest went okay, but I was only in the cow pen for a minute before their incessant mooing started to get on my nerves. My head hurts and there is so much left to do.

10:05am

The mooing is even louder and making my head hurt. I hate farming.

4:30pm

Finally, I've done all the chores. I can't wait to get back to the mines tomorrow.

6:45pm

Steve is so annoying! He came home showing off his finds for the day: a saddle, more diamonds and a few things I'd never seen before. He decided to show the animals too. Doesn't he see their bored faces?

The diamonds did seem to catch the cows' interest. They actually stopped mooing. I would have liked that saddle. I heard you can saddle up a pig and ride them round the farm. That would be kind of funny.

6:48pm

Steve said I can't borrow his saddle... ever. Mining Steve is no more fun than Farming Steve. He can go back to harvesting tomorrow.

9:50pm

I went for a late night walk around the farm and was attacked by a baby zombie. How are those things so fast? I struck it about a hundred times with my sword. Finally, the little terror dropped some flesh and orbs. I hope that run-in doesn't give me more nightmares.

Day Twenty-One

7:45am

I couldn't find Steve this morning. He wasn't outside or in the kitchen. Finally, I checked his bed and found a sign reading "Until further notice, you harvest, I mine. Since when is he the boss?

Oh yeah! According to him, it's because he was here first, as he always reminds me. I hate harvesting. I hope Steve falls down a mine shaft.

10:00am

Feeling grumpy, I killed all but two of our cows. I didn't re-breed them either. Take that, Steve.

10:30am

I felt bad for the cows, so I gave them some wheat. Baby cows are pretty cute. Know who isn't cute? Steve.

1:12pm

I planted new seeds for wheat. I cooked all the beef. Thank you, cows. I collected wool from the sheep.

I did everything. I always do everything. Steve is useless. He needs to fall in a hole.

5:00pm

Remember when Steve was nice and showed me how to mine? No? Me neither.

When he came home, he gloated about a shiny new set of horse armor. Where did he find that and what is the point? He doesn't even have a horse!

5:15pm

At dinner I gathered the courage to ask Steve why he wasn't letting me mine. He patted my back and said the he was better at mining and I was better at the farm stuff. He didn't even blink when I hurled my potato across the room , stormed off to my bedroom and slammed the door. He can't get away with this!

10:45pm

Can't sleep. Too mad at Steve. I have to do something about him once and for all.

11:00pm

Thinking about how I threw the potato starting chuckling to myself under the covers. I must have looked ridiculous. Maybe I shouldn't be such a baby about the whole thing.

Day Twenty-Two

2:00am

I am not being a baby. Steve is being unfair. I decided that I need to teach him a lesson.

3:07am

I quietly practiced my evil laugh, because I have hatched an evil-genius plan. Using obsidian to surround a water hole, I will push Steve in and seal the top with more of that unbreakable rock.

He won't be able to escape and then I will be able to mine whenever I please. I chuckled as I imagined him being forced to re-spawn, waking up in bed, realizing he lost everything.

8:45am

As Steve headed to the mine, I stealthily follow close behind. He is oblivious.

Once I get down in the mines with him, I will go off on my own to collect some obsidian. I need to get home before Steve does or he'll know something's up.

3:45pm

Made it home minutes before Steve. I had finished my farming chores before he woke up this morning so that he'd think I'd been there all day. While he put away all of his precious mining treasures from today, I went to work. I built a hole surrounded with obsidian next to the pig pen. Those fat pink pigs blinked with wondering eyes as I worked. They probably thought I was crazy. They won't miss Steve though. Who would?

It's time to put my plan into play. I can feel my evil side getting excited. I need a better evil laugh for times like this.

4:30pm

I fail at life.

My plan was working perfectly until Steve ruined it. I lured him to the hole, saying that I thought the pigs were escaping. When he got near the hole, I said "Would you look at that weird hole!" Then, as he peered into the water-filled hole, I pretended to fall into him.

As Steve plunged in the water, I shoved the block of obsidian over the top. "Oops!" I said, "Clumsy me!"

Then, I backed up a little to see if it worked.

Next thing I knew, Steve burst through the top block with a diamond pickaxe! Where was he carrying that? His pocket? His shoe? Wouldn't that hurt?

I tried to brush off the incident by saying that I meant to break the rock, not lay the rock. I think he bought it. Anyway, I hope he did.

10:00pm

I avoided eye contact with Steve for the rest of the night. If he guesses my plans, that would be the worst.

11:45pm

I need get my rest and make sure to be smarter tomorrow -- way smarter.

Day Twenty-Three

5:00am

Maybe I can have someone else kill Steve for me. Then it wouldn't be my fault. Plenty of mobs clutter the landscape with no better use for their evil skills. I can't use skeletons, because they will kill me before I can even ask. Spiders are too weak. Steve would slay them in minutes and come home flaunting their string and eye balls. Maybe a zombie or creeper could be convinced with the right approach. How hard can it be?

5:30am

My iron armor still fits. Good! Now I need to arm myself with some bravery to match.

5:35am

I started thinking about last time I tried talking to mobs and nearly fainted back into my bed. I got back up and gave myself a pep talk. It won't be like last time. It won't be like last time. I am more evil and braver than ever before!

I let another one of those evil donkey laughs escape...
I've got to get that fixed.

5:40am

I am not brave.

5:43am

Enough! I screwed my courage to the sticking point
and went off to scout out some evil pros.

6:00am

I attempted conversation with to a creeper. Bad idea!
Creepers are not chatty. I walked up to one in the
field and got as far as "Excuse me, would you be
willing...?" His face went all white and blinky, and
then came the "Ssssssss!"

The impatient creeper wouldn't even hear me out! I
escaped before he exploded, but only barely before.
Damage forced me to take a break and chow down
some steak for my hearts to re-fill. I don't feel sorry
for them anymore. You want to blow yourself up for
no reason, fine by me!

I won't do that again. Those guys are just mean. Like
Steve.

6:30am

I spied a lone zombie. One zombie would be easier to approach than a crowd. My mind was muddled though, and I struggled to gather my thoughts. It didn't go so well last time.

It didn't go well this time either. I snuck up behind the zombie. His creepy, loud groaning melted my courage. "Be brave," I reminded myself. "Zombie guy," I said with my chest puffed out like Steve does when he is acting tough, "any chance you want to help me? I need Steve out of my life I would like you to do it for me."

He turned and blinked. And then he chased me! I swatted at him with my sword and managed to kill him. I returned depressed, with zombie flesh is now rotting in my pockets.

I haven't given up, though. Not yet.

9:15am

The endermen are lurking today. I wonder if I can convince them to kill Steve. Could I even bear to approach one? I can't even look into the eyes of one of those freaky things.

9:18am

I remembered that Steve told me to a pumpkin on your head to keep endermen from hurting you. Was he serious? It sounds ridiculous, but it might be worth a try. I hollowed out a pumpkin and then plopped it over my head. I must look like I've lost my mind. I couldn't help but think that my final memories in life will be viewed from the slimy inside of a pumpkin. Fantastic…

I managed to summon a not-so-evil evil laugh. It has given me a little courage.

9:25am

Nope. These guys are scary. Forget it. I am going back to bed.

9:26am

The enderman appeared right as I turned for home. A weird sound gurgled from its throat, almost causing me to bolt. I choked out, "Here's a diamond. Kill Steve for me. Okay?" I mouth felt strange as I said this, like all my teeth were loose. The enderman took the diamond. For a moment, I felt frozen to the spot where I stood. But I finally came to my senses and ran for it.

9:30am

I, Alex, am still alive! I can't believe that worked. I punched the air, pumped my fist and did a happy dance. All I need now is for Steve to go outside.

10:00am

Please, Steve, stop staring at your cat, and go outside!!

10:05am

Trying to distract myself with a book to keep from thinking about how he still hasn't gone outside.

10:07am

Is he going to stay home today? What if the enderman has already teleported away with the diamond?

10:15am

Finally! Steve is going outside. No turning back now…

10:20am

The enderman has Steve backed up against the wall. Steve looks scared enough to melt into a puddle.

Yes, yes, yes! He is going to kill Steve.

10:21am

Steve smote the enderman with his sword making the enderman disappear. Unfortunately, he re-appeared where Steve could see him. Steve killed him in seconds. I'm now out one diamond and still stuck with Steve. I fail at life.

10:25am

Steve ran back into the house and called me. When I showed up, he was grinning and holding ender pearls, so proud of himself for killing the enderman. Steve thinks he is so awesome… I think I might barf.

11:00am

The ender pearls are kind of cool. I snuck into Steve's room to have a look at them. I would never admit to him that they are neat, because it would go to his head. I wondered for a moment if he would notice if I took them.

Of course he would notice! He wouldn't stop going on about them and how he wants to use them to teleport all around the biomes. Big deal! Just use your feet, Steve.

12:30pm

Steve is still bragging about how great he is. I am sick of him replaying the moves of the fight, showing off his sword swinging and bragging how brave he is. He said he will teach me how to kill endermen.

1:00pm

Steve needs to fall in a hole.

7:30pm

I spent all afternoon trying to figure out what to do about Steve while I tackled the farm duties. Steve is right. I am way better at farming and harvesting than he is, but it doesn't mean I like it. I want to be searching dark caves for diamonds, digging up gold for making golden apples, and bravely fighting off poisonous spiders.

Well… Maybe not that last part.

Every time I try to get rid of Steve, I fail. I need a foolproof plan. Something he will never see coming.

7:45pm

Steve came into my room and showed me how he teleports with the ender pearls. He moved across the room in a blink. I still don't see what the big deal is.

Wow... you're awesome, buddy. Steve needs to teleport into a hole.

Wait... Maybe that is the answer. Steve needs to disappear into a hole -- for real! But how?

Day Twenty-Four

5:00am

I spent the night imagining pushing Steve into a hole all night but couldn't figure out how. No matter what, he will see me coming. I am going to head out today and wander the fields. Maybe if I clear my head, Steve won't bug me as much. I can hope, right.

10:20am

I was wandering in the fields and practicing my evil laugh. Sometimes it relaxes me to think about how evil I could be. My laugh still sounds too much like a donkey -- so much so that one came running up to me as I was laughing. My awful evil hee-haw laugh attracts donkeys! This means I really have a lot of work to do before it sounds like a real evil villainous laugh.

10:30am

Why didn't I think of using my laugh sooner? Steve will never see it coming. Tomorrow, I will load Steve up on a donkey and lure the donkey right over a cliff. All the armor and saddles in the world won't help him! Oh, I really am evil.

Maybe my laugh was always meant to help me. I shall embrace my donkeylike noises. This is going to work, I know it!

1:00pm

Steve came home for lunch today. He never comes home for lunch. I had to hide my evil smile from him. He's been suspicious ever since I pushed him in the watery pit. Hoping to avoid future attempts on his life perhaps, He talked about how great I am at farming and how much he appreciates all I do. Blah, blah, blah! Enjoy your donkey ride, Steve!

3:00pm

I did it. I snuck Steve's sadly out to the pigsty and saddled up a pig! I rode good old Charlie all the way to the nearest cliff's edge to search for hiding spots. To keep the pig moving, I had to dangle a carrot off of a fishing rod just in front of its nose.

3:15pm

We got to the cliff sooner than expected. I was lost and thought and the pig was focused on the carrot. We found ourselves riding right over the cliff's edge. I thought I was headed for a respawn for sure, but the craziest thing happened! Charlie flew! Oh man, we had a ball flying around. I am not telling Steve about this... ever!

I got home just before Steve and had enough time to put Charlie back into his pen, and the saddle back in Steve's chest. Over dinner, I told Steve I had a present for him -- his very own donkey to ride. I said I found it in the woods by our place while looking for mushrooms for soup.

He seemed to love the present. He said he could use the donkey to carry loads to and from the mines. I hadn't even thought of that, but I said that was exactly why I brought him the donkey. He just had to comment, though, that a horse would have been better. Why can't he just be nice and grateful?

6:15pm

Steve is lazy. He didn't even collect and restack the bowls from dinner. I wish I lived with anyone else.

8:00pm

The house is finally clean. I went around and picked up everything and put it back in its place and it took forever. Steve didn't even say thank you. He just corrected me when I tried to put things in the "wrong" chests. I can't wait for tomorrow.

10:30pm

I can't sleep. I'm too excited. I guess I'll spend the night practicing my donkey laugh.

11:45pm

Steve came to ask what all the noise was about in my room. Guess my laughs were louder than I thought. Oops. Go back to bed, Steve.

11:47pm

Yep, I'm still practicing too loudly. The donkey I brought Steve is now staring into my bedroom window.

Day Twenty-Five

8:00am

Today's the day! I decided to wear all leather armor today to blend in with the trees. It's not the most protective, but it will help conceal me. I am brilliant.
8:01
In my excitement, I decided to practice my evil laugh. The donkey is back at my window. Stupid donkey!

8:45am

Steve just woke up. It's time to get moving.

12:45pm

I managed to stay ahead of Steve but out of sight the whole way through the woods. The donkey sounds were working, and I got Steve and his donkey to the cliff just past Steve's mining spot. I just need him to stay on that donkey!

He is just about at the cliff. Steve is confused. The donkey won't listen to him. But he isn't getting off. I am so close I can taste victory!

At the cliff, there wasn't anywhere to hide, but I jumped a couple blocks down into the deep ravine and screamed the loudest donkey laugh that I could.

Before Steve arrived at the cliff, it was just my luck that every single donkey in existence came first. The cavern started filling with falling donkeys chasing my noises minutes before Steve showed up. By the time he arrived, the cavern was full of hee-hawing bodies. I fail at life!

When I tried to escape the ravine myself, I was trampled by all of the donkeys also trying to flee the deep space. Now, I have black eyes, sore ribs and a bruised ego.

I punched everything I could reach the whole way home: trees, grass, animals, even flowers for goodness' sake. I hurt my hands hitting the trees. I can never do anything right. I can't even punch right.

When I got home, Steve was already there. I pretended I was getting back from a walk in the field and hid my face so he couldn't see the hoof imprints on my forehead. He didn't even notice.

Steve told me all about his donkey going crazy and leading him, along with a million other donkeys, into a ravine. He said he wished I could have seen how insane it looked.

I saw it, Steve. You should have fallen, too. Lucky you, Steve. Unlucky me.

2:00pm

I want to wallow in bed in my self-pity, but of course, it's still day. You cannot sleep until night time.

2:15pm

What to do? What to do? My face looks completely insane -- all puffy and black and blue. I want to hurt all the donkeys, but only slightly less than I want to hurt Steve. How am I going to do that?

3:30pm

I am going to dig a hole. I am literally going to push Steve into a hole. That's what he deserves, right?

8:30pm

Once Steve is asleep, I am digging a hole.

10:00pm

I almost died. The world is against me. It's not fair.

I dug a really deep hole -- about 14 blocks deep. When I slammed my pickaxe against the stone under me, lava started to bubble up. It burnt me! Ouch! Lava is unbearably hot. No one tells you that.

I jumped up and placed a cobblestone block just below my feet. I am so useless. The ladder I built was just long enough to get me out. I broke it behind me so Steve has no way to escape.

Steve won't survive this fall. No way. It's a long way down, and it makes me feel wobbly. Oh, I felt dizzy!

"Don't barf, Alex," I told myself.

10:05pm

I didn't barf. Came close, but I walked back into the house and went to my room. Wish me luck tomorrow.

Day Twenty-Six

12:00pm

Steve was gone before I got up today. I spent all morning pacing nervously between the farm animals and the house. Twice I almost fell into the hole I dug. Twice!

2:30pm

I did the chores as quickly as I could. Steve can't know anything is weird. He still isn't back. What could be taking him so long?
Never mind, here he comes. More later.

3:00pm

Steve demanded an early dinner and called my mushroom soup disgusting. He sent me out to collect two chickens and cook them. He is grumpy, or maybe hangry. His hunger bars are pretty low.

4:00pm

He ate both chickens! What am I supposed to eat? He is still grumpy, too. What reason does he have to be grumpy? He gets to mine his diamonds and even craft with them. If there is anyone who should be happy, it's Steve. Steve needs to die.

4:44pm

I ate a couple apples I had stored to turn gold. My hunger isn't satisfied, but it will have to do. It's time to push Steve in a hole. My evil laugh is busting to get out.

4:45pm

My evil laugh slipped out real quick. It felt good.

4:46pm

Steve just asked me if I heard a donkey.

Note to self: Evil laugh still needs major improvements.

5:30pm

I HATE CREEPERS! They ruin everything! Why did I ever feel sorry for those wandering psychopaths?

I called Steve outside and said I found some iron ore not too far down for him to mine. He didn't even wonder why I wouldn't mine it for myself. That is how selfish he is. But, before he could get to the hole, a nosey creeper wandered over. He got right next to me before I noticed him, and the next thing I knew, I had fallen bottom first and it hurt something awful. The creeper exploded right at edge of the hole!

Steve wandered over and climbed into the explosion hole. The vanished creeper caused a hole leading straight to a huge cluster of iron ore. Seriously! How does this happen? Steve collected all the iron, said thank you to me and climbed out with a goofy grin on his face.

I hate Steve. I hate that creeper. I hate my life. I give up. I can't kill Steve, he is just too lucky.

1:00am

I am too useless to fall asleep.

Day Twenty-Seven

10:05am

Steve barged in while I was wallowing in pity in my room. I didn't want to see his face today. He came to show me the iron sword and armor he made from the iron ore he mined yesterday.

Stupid creeper hole.

He enchanted the sword with sharpness and anti-breakage spells. To make his new armor extra strong, he also enchanted it all with anti-breakage spells as well as fire protection. He spun around to show me everything and asked if I thought it was cool. I managed a nod.

Steve is such a show-off. Just as he was walking out of my room, he turned and said "Don't you think I am awesome, Alex?" Oh Steve, I think you are just the most awesome. Not!

10:10am

I changed my mind. I don't give up. Steve needs to go. I will do everything I can to get rid of him. I can't quite. The world will be better with no Steve! I've had enough of this showboat attitude.

2:45pm

Thinking of ways to kill Steve has distracted me so that I keep messing up. I forgot to breed the pigs, tried to give the sheep carrots and attempted to sheer a cow. It took me twice as long to get everything done, and I still haven't come up with any kind of new plan to get rid of Steve. I am the worst evil villain there ever was.

3:00pm

Noticed that I left the cow pen open and all the baby cows escaped. I had to breed them all over again. Focus, Alex, focus! Today is a bad day.

5:00pm

What if I build a nether portal and trick Steve into going in? I doubt he could survive the Nether.

5:30pm

Turns out Steve has been to the Nether and loved it. He told me that is how he has a brewing stand. He went to the Nether and killed a blaze. I will never have a brewing stand. I am way too scared to go to the Nether. He said he would love to take me to the Nether and show me around. Umm… no, thank you. I've heard stories. The Nether is a dangerous place, and I am not that brave.

6:00pm

I purposely fed Steve mushroom soup again. He did not like it. His face was hilarious as he tried to swallow the soup. He asked me to stop making it, but if Steve doesn't like it he can make his own dinner. I said that to him, too. He just frowned. Yeah. Take that! It made my day at least a tiny bit better. I like torturing Steve.

7:00pm

It's almost bedtime and I will have to live through another day of Steve's lame stories and Steve's know-it-all attitude unless I can think of something.

8:00pm

Think, Alex.

10:45pm

My brain hurts. Too much thinking.

Day Twenty-Eight

6:00am

I fell asleep thinking; I woke up thinking, and I have gotten nowhere. I am so tired.

11:00am

Sometimes, the brain just needs a sweaty walk in the desert. A smart idea popped into my head as I traded with the desert villagers in the desert biome closest to our place.

A long time ago, Steve and I found this village – the only village with an Iron Golem, because of the village's size. That is why we built so close by -- endless trade and a short commute!

Supposedly, the Iron Golem protects the villagers against anything trying to hurt them. If this is the case, that big iron beast will try to kill Steve if he hurts a villager. All I have to figure out is how to make him hurt a villager.

11:15am

Three laps around the village and I have my answer. Steve loves his diamonds, but gets extremely angry when villagers want to trade five emeralds for one diamond. He has threatened to kill them for this poor trade before. I will tell him about a villager trying to sell me diamonds for too few emeralds.

I've asked a villager to make this trade with me, and promised him I would go through with the trade later. "Hhhrrrmm," he responded. I hope that means "Yes."

11:17am

I laughed evil donkey laughs all the way home. A donkey ran up and licked my face. He appeared out of nowhere! I fail at evil laughing and at life.

5:00pm

It's time to rock and roll on out of here. I told Steve about the trade and his face went red. I said I would lead him to the villager who dared to be so foolish. I feel pretty evil right now!

8:30pm

What is the term for correct term for waking up re-spawned in your bed?

Oh yeah – "Failure!"

It's a long story what happened with the villager. I will start with trip to the village. Steve was so mad he pulled out his sword before we even hit the desert. For once I thought this may actually work. Steve may be angry enough to get himself killed. I should not have gotten excited.

We got to the village as the sun was going down. When it sank behind the hills, hordes of zombies surrounded the village. There were adult zombies, villager zombies and so many babies. I have never seen so many of them!

Steve and I both fought off the zombies alongside the Iron Golem. It's all a little blurry, but I turned and hit what I thought was a zombie -- only it wasn't. I straight up hurt a villager baby!

The Iron Golem didn't miss a beat. He wailed on me. I had no chance.

Now, here I am in bed, dazed and confused again.

9:00pm

Steve just came in to ask if I was all right. He said he killed four more zombies after I left. Then, he built a fence around the village and put another Iron Golem on guard. He asked me why I hurt a baby villager. It's not as if I meant too, Steve.

Day Twenty-Nine

8:30am

Steve just left for the day. I am going to go through his stuff and see if there is anything I can use against him.

10:30am

Steve has a whole chest filled with just diamonds. Seriously, he can't share? Come on! In another chest I found all kinds of dyed wool. The art I could craft with that would be mind-blowing. I am starting to think Steve may be a hoarder. He never uses any of this stuff, and he has some crazy stuff, like 64 pieces of zombie flesh. Why? Maybe I should get him help.

Nah! He is too proud. He would never accept help.

11:00am

Ooh! I found invisibility potion!

11:05am

And a diamond sword!

11:07am

I can use these beautiful creations, but I have to leave them in Steve's room until I am ready to use them. I can't have him notice anything missing. I don't know why I didn't think of this before. I am going to drink the invisibility potion and then hit Steve with the sword until he dies. It's that simple.

1:40pm

I wish I could nap. I need to be full strength before I kill Steve. I will wait until morning and hope I sleep some tonight.

2:30pm

I hate harvesting and farming. It is so boring! Not to mention I am constantly on the lookout for dangers. Why didn't Steve enclose this place better? He isn't as smart as he thinks he is. Around the pens and fields, I would have built high stone walls with iron doors operated with redstone switches. I know how to keep things secure.

Farming puts me in such a bad mood. If we could switch places, I would be so much happier. But that would require Steve to be nice, and that never happens. He just has to die. I see no other way around it.

6:00pm

I almost threw my potato at Steve's head during supper. He started going on about killing that enderman again. Do I really need to hear this story five hundred times? He needs someone new to talk to about his stories. I have had enough. His face annoys me.

6:15pm

Imagine how great it would have been if I had hit him with my hot potato. Oh, man! I would have laughed so hard! That might make me almost as mean as him, but I think I have reasons to be mean and to want Steve gone.

Reasons Steve Needs To Die:

He brags all the time. All the time!

He is messy. Leaves leather pants lying around everywhere.

He doesn't share anything. Ever!

He doesn't cook, but he complains about the cooking.

He won't farm.

He laughs when I get hurt. Not funny!

He is rude.

He thinks he is the best at everything.

I am sure I could think of more if I wanted to, but I don't want the list to cloud my thoughts any more than it already has. The point is that he is an all-round awful human. Not that I am amazing, but at least I show appreciation for nice things, and I try not to brag.

10:30pm

While Steve went outside to cut a little wood for some project, I stole the invisibility potion and the sword. I hid them in my chest for the morning and hoped he wouldn't notice.

When he came back inside, I asked him not to leave before I got up the next day. When he questioned why, I told him that I wanted him to teach me some fighting moves. Of course, that worked. Steve is so predictable. I should add that to the list.

Day Thirty

8:00am

It feels good to be well-rested. I tried to count sheep to fall asleep, but we only have ten sheep so I quickly ran out. However, I drifted off thinking of life without Steve. It would be a little lonely having no one to talk to, but the donkeys seem to listen to me a little, so maybe I would have one move into the house.

\I could mine all morning and farm before bed. I'd make cool things and build huge structures. Maybe I would even move to a village and enjoy noisy village life. At least they don't brag. Life could be pretty nice.

8:15am

I drank the invisibility potion. It tasted like fermented spider eyes. Don't ask how I would know that.

8:30am

Steve called me but had no idea I was right behind him. An evil laugh just about slipped out of my mouth. Choking it back caused me to regurgitate a bit of potion, which almost started a coughing fit. I ran back to my room to catch a breath. Close call!

9:45am

I'm terrible at everything. My plan failed and now Steve knows for sure now that I have been trying to kill him.

I left my room earlier and pulled out my sword behind Steve. He was still looking for me to teach me his lame fighting moves. Just as I lifted my diamond beauty into the air to swing at him, the potion ran out. Steve backed up and ran me through me with his sword!

I just woke up, re-spawned, in bed. Steve came in and hovered over me with a repentant look on his face. He apologized. He said he didn't realize it was me until it was too late. I don't know whether I believe him.

Steve said he noticed me losing patience lately and thought maybe I could use a few mining days here and there. I scowled at him.

"How about every other day? That's the best I can do," he offered. I agreed. I was still skeptical. He said that as part of the deal, I have to stop trying to kill him.

"No promises!" I muttered as he left the room.

Day Thirty-One

7:00am

Today is a brand new day. I am packed up and ready to head off mining. Steve made me breakfast and gave me some cooked fish to take for lunch. He promised he will try and be nicer, but he still bragged about how well he cooked the fish. Some things will never change.

11:00am

It feels so good to be down here in the dim light of the mine shaft. I haven't found much, but I can't stop smiling. Maybe this is all I need to forgive Steve: a little freedom and a lot less farming. With any luck we will work things out after all. Maybe I am just not made to be evil. Positive thoughts!

12:30pm

I had leftovers from breakfast for my lunch. Okay, I will hand it to Steve, the fish was pretty delicious!

To be continued…

Made in the USA
Coppell, TX
09 December 2024

42077453R00036